GIRAFFES CAN'T DANCE

Giles Andreae
Guy Parker-Rees

Gerald was a tall giraffe

Whose neck was long and slim,

But his knees were awfully bandy

And his legs were rather thin.

He was very good at standing still

And munching shoots off trees,

But when he tried to run around

He buckled at the knees.

Now every year
in Africa

They hold the
Jungle Dance,

Where every single animal

Turns up to skip and prance.

And this year when the day arrived
the day arrived

Poor Gerald felt so sad,

Because when it came to dancing

He was really very bad.

The warthogs started waltzing

And the rhinos rock 'n' rolled

The lions danced
a tango

Which was elegant
and bold.

The chimps all did a cha-cha

With a very latin feel,

And eight baboons
then teamed up

For a splendid
Scottish reel.

Gerald swallowed bravely

As he walked towards the floor,

But the lions saw him coming

And they soon began to roar.

"Hey, look at clumsy Gerald," The animals all laughed,

"Giraffes can't dance, you silly fool,

Oh Gerald, don't be daft!"

Gerald simply froze up,
He was rooted to the spot.

"They're right," he thought, "I'm useless,

Oh, I feel like such a clot."

So he crept off from the dancefloor

And he started walking home,

He'd never felt so sad before

So sad and so alone.

Then he found a little clearing

And he looked up at the sky,

"The moon can be so beautiful,"
He whispered with a sigh.

"Excuse me!" coughed a cricket Who'd seen Gerald earlier on,

"But sometimes when you're different

You just need a different song."

"Listen to the swaying grass
And listen to the trees,

To me the sweetest music

Is those branches in the breeze.

"So imagine that that lovely moon

Is playing just for you,

Everything makes music

If you really want it to."

With that, the cricket smiled

And picked up his violin.

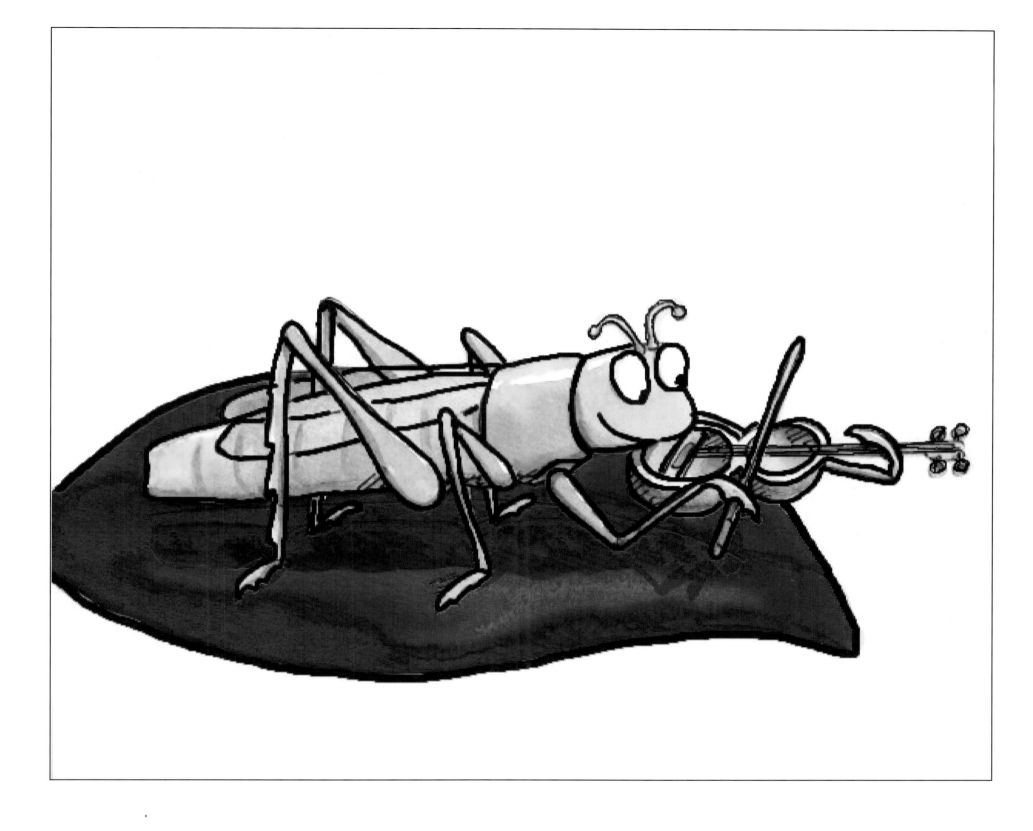

Then Gerald felt his body

Do the most amazing thing.

His hooves had started shuffling

Making circles on the ground,

His neck was gently swaying

And his tail was swishing round.

He threw his arms out sideways

And he swung them everywhere,

Then he did a backwards somersault

And leapt up in the air.

Gerald felt so wonderful

His mouth was open wide,

"I am dancing!
Yes, I'm dancing!

I AM DANCING!"
Gerald cried.

Then one by one
each animal

Who'd been there
at the dance

Arrived while Gerald boogied on

And watched him quite entranced.

They shouted,
"It's a miracle!

We must be in a dream,

Gerald's the best dancer

That we've ever ever seen!"

"How is it you can dance like that? Please, Gerald, tell us how."

But Gerald simply twizzled round

And finished with a bow.

Then he raised his head and looked up

At the moon and stars above.

"We all can dance," he said,

"When we find music that we love."

THE END

Giraffes Can't Dance

First published 1999 by Orchard Books

Author Giles Andreae

Text © Purple Enterprises 1999

Illustrations © Guy Parker-Rees

Giant Print & Braille edition

Published in 2014 by Access2Books

www.access2books.org

ISBN 987-1909225-37-4